# This Books Belongs to

# Find Us On

**Website** www.adropfromeden.com

**Instagram** https://www.instagram.com/adropfromeden/

**Twitter  https://twitter.com/adropfromeden**

**Facebook aromatherapy group** https://
www.facebook.com/groups/adropfromeden

**Facebook Ministry Group** https://www.facebook.com/
groups/adropfromedenministry

# About the Author

Hello Everyone, my name is Felicia Patterson. I am an author, and minister, have a master's in aromatherapy and skincare, and am a psychology major. I was born with a rare spinal and immune deficiency that made physically going to school impossible. For this reason, I was hospital homebound from birth. My parents homeschooled me until I surpassed them, then did a combination of virtual education and having teachers sent to my home. This experience inspired me to create content that both helps achieve common core standards while making learning fun. Being the youngest of six whom did brick and mortar education. I fully believe that being home-taught not only gave me a much better education, the ability to achieve things faster, to be self-disciplined, and a free thinker, but

also a life perspective that most don't have.

# HOW TO USE THIS BOOK

1— Find a story starter that attracts you the most.
2— figure out what you are doing in the story, how you got into the situation and how you will end the story.
3— Start Writing!

---

Remember! It's your story.
Use your imagination and live in it.
Make the characters animals , aliens or superheros, and give them names.
You can also move the story starter to the middle or end of your story.
Again you are the boss,
change the settings however you want.

# A strange spaceship just crashed and landed in your backyard. What happens next?

**Make up a story about where thunder comes from.**

# If you could add any class to your school schedule, what would it be?

**Finish the story: Once upon a time, there was a dragon...**

# Write about a special bond you have with an animal.

**Write a letter to your teacher telling them why your favorite book should be studied in class.**

**Write an alternative ending for your favorite book or movie.**

# Describe a day in your life if you were famous.

# If you could be famous for anything, what would it be?

# Write a story that takes place in a forest.

# Write a story about a volcano that's about to erupt.

**Write a story that includes the sentence, "I should have seen this coming."**

**Write a silly or scary story to tell around a campfire.**

**If you could write a book about anything, what would you write about?**

**A strange spaceship just crashed and landed in your backyard. What happens next?**

**Write a story about what you think your parents were like when they were younger.**

**Write a recommendation of a book or movie for a friend. Why do you think they would enjoy it?**

**Pick a partner and write a story together! Start by writing the first sentence, then pass it to your partner to write the second sentence.**

**Write a story where two people meet in an unusual way and become fast friends.**

# What is your earliest memory? Describe it in as much detail as you can remember

# Write a "quarantine story

**Write a story about a journey at sea.**

**Write about a famous person and why you admire them.**

**Your pet is in charge of you for a day. What will they make
you do?**

**Write a story where someone discovers something they aren't supposed to know**

**You're the host of a new game show. Write about what happens in the first episode.**

**If there was a magical portal in the back of your closet, where would it lead to?**

**Write a story about a magical hat. Where is it from? What does it do? What does it look like?**

**You find buried treasure in the park, hidden in a big wooden chest. What kind of treasure is it? Who left it there?**

**Write a sympathetic story from the point of view of the "bad guy." (Think fractured fairy tales like *Wicked* or *The True Story of the 3 Little Pigs!*, although the story doesn't have to be a fairy tale.)**

**Imagine you are chosen for the first mission to Mars. What would you bring with you, and what do you think exploring the planet would be like?**

**Write a story where one character must keep an important secret. Will it be discovered?**

**You're a wildlife photographer trying to get a photo of a rare animal. What animal is it and how will you find it?**

**You're a detective working on a big, important case. What is it and how do you solve it?**

**Every year a new person is sent to the moon, and now it's your turn. What happens when you step out of the rocket?**

**Write a story where all your favorite characters from books and movies meet up. What do they get up to?**

**Pretend you are a professional reviewer and write a review of a book you recently read or a TV show/movie you recently watched. How many stars would you give it? What did you like about it, and what didn't you like?**

**You get sucked into the pages of your favorite book. What happens when you join the story?**

**Write a story where a boring, everyday experience gets turned into a big adventure.**

**There's an old house at the end of the street hidden behind tall, dark trees. No one has been brave enough to enter, until now...**

# Write a story about a family that can travel in time.

**you just joined a super-secret spy organization. What's your first mission?**

**Boom, you're a superhero! Give yourself an origin story, describe your superpowers and plan what you'll do to make the world a better place**

**Your house has a secret and mysterious history. Write a story about what happened before you lived there.**

**You get transported into the last video game you played.**

**Where are you?**

________________________________________________

________________________________________________

________________________________________________

________________________________________________

________________________________________________

________________________________________________

________________________________________________

________________________________________________

________________________________________________

________________________________________________

________________________________________________

________________________________________________

________________________________________________

________________________________________________

**You've got the wrong person – it wasn't me!" Continue this story…**